anythink

D0575364

NO LONGER PROPERTY OF ANYTHINK RANGEVIEW LIBRARY DISTRICT

anythink

Can You
See Me?

To Teddy

Copyright © 2019 by Bob Staake

All rights reserved.
Published in the United States by Random House Children's Books,
a division of Penguin Random House LLC, New York.

Beginner Books, Random House, and the Random House colophon
are registered trademarks of Penguin Random House LLC.

The Cat in the Hat logo ® and © Dr. Seuss Enterprises, L.P. 1957,
renewed 1986. All rights reserved.

Visit us on the Web!
rhcbooks.com

Educators and librarians, for a variety of teaching tools, visit us at
RHTeachersLibrarians.com

Library of Congress Cataloging-in-Publication Data
Names: Staake, Bob, author, illustrator.
Title: Can you see me? / by Bob Staake.
Description: First Edition. | New York : Beginner Books, a division of Random House, [2018] |
Summary: A giant lizard takes a colorful approach to blending in with his surroundings
and hiding from a group of children.
Identifiers: LCCN 2017037790 (print) | LCCN 2017051780 (ebook) | ISBN 978-0-385-37315-9 (trade) |
ISBN 978-0-375-97197-6 (lib. bdg.) | ISBN 978-0-375-98188-3 (ebook)
Subjects: | CYAC: Stories in rhyme. | Lizards—Fiction. | Camouflage (Biology)—Fiction.
Classification: LCC PZ8.3.S778 (ebook) | LCC PZ8.3.S778 Can 2018 (print) | DDC [E]—dc23

Printed in the United States of America
10 9 8 7 6 5 4 3 2 1
First Edition

Random House Children's Books supports the First Amendment
and celebrates the right to read.

Can You See Me?

by Bob Staake

BEGINNER BOOKS®
A Division of Random House

I am yellow.

Now I'm pink.

ONE WAY

INK
INC.

Now I am
as black as ink!

Can you find me
in this tree?
I'm leafy green
and hard to see.

Take a look.

I have a trick.

I'm red—just like
a wall of brick!

Hey there! Hi there!
Now I'm blue.

I'm swimming with
a kangaroo.

I'm white.

(Too bright!)

Then dark
as night.

Can you find me
way up high?
I'm hiding in
the cloudy sky!

We can see you
hiding there!
We can see you
ANYwhere!

I'm orange!
I'm brown!

I'm all over town!

Purple tulips,
roses, too,
hide me in a place
that's new!

I'm checkered
in squares.
I'm hiding
on stairs.

I'm inside
a box.
I'm gray like
the rocks!

From my head
to my foot
I'm covered
in soot.

The rain makes me clean. . . .

Hey, LOOK!

Now I'm green!

Can you see me
in the store?
I'm hiding near
the yellow door!

Fresh Frui

We can see you
hiding there!
We can see you
ANYwhere!

I'm as gold as the wheat.

I'm a peppermint sweet!

LOOK OUT! Now I'm violet—
a daredevil pilot!

Then with
a balloon . . .

. . . I'm off
to the MOON!

But I'll
return soon.